Genetic Nightmare

Book One

Of

The Bio Wars Saga

By

Timothy Gibbs

&

Guy Lozier

Genetic Nightmare

Published in the USA by

Seventh Sense Publishing

Cover Illustration by Guy Lozier

Cover Design by Guy Lozier & Kayla Delgado

Printed in the United States of America

Genetic Nightmare

OTHER BOOKS
by
GUY LOZIER

The Mindrift Saga
The Eternal: Guardian of Light
The Morantian

The Disclosure Files
Assassinating Custer
The Hybrid Anunnaki

The Millennial Cycles
Menazia Reborn

The Bio Wars Saga
Genetic Nightmare

The Great Dragons Series
Dragon Destiny

Universal Conquest
The 7th Sense
Building the 7th Sense

Anthologies

What Lurks in Darkness
Secrets
Detours Through Liminal Space
Illuminated

OTHER BOOKS TO BE RELEASED SOON
by
GUY LOZIER

The Indie Matrix

The Indie Matrix – Book 1

BioTank Series

TankMaster Bronson – Book 1

The Mindrift Saga

The Darklanders

The Disclosure Files

The Infinity Principle

The Dark Heros Saga

Dante

The T.L.R. Group
Growing UP Mayberry – Just the Facts

Acknowledgement

Without our wives and close friends, we could never have accomplished publishing our story.

Dedication

Mary Kathryn Roland Hall, grandmother of Timothy Gibbs, has been a powerful influence in Timothy's life. It is our loved ones around us that make us stronger, explained Guy Lozier.

Genetic Nightmare

CHAPTER ONE

Through science man will discover the very walls of his prison...

Sparks

The decisions were final. All divisions would be pulled from Earth's oversight. Only one group would continue to oversee operations. With Earth's leaders pursuing aggressive particle weapons, it was just too dangerous to continue to protect Earth any longer. All colonies would be withdrawn to a safe distance, then carefully planned patrols would assist but with limited interaction. At least until humans learned their lesson. While this might mean much of the planet could be damaged or destroyed, the lesson was necessary for the human evolutionary path.

Our people had watched over humans for thousands of years. Our leaders had spent many of the recent decades attempting to assist the human evolutionary outcomes but only by offering to assist with positive advancements. Human leaders would have nothing to do with it, preferring weapons over removal of diseases, military applications over economic equality and stabilization, overbearing eavesdropping of oppression on the population over transparency of government, and the list just went on and on. All the old lower vibratory 3D issues: rape, pillage, greed, and power. Sampling of the population showed that the majority of humans did not agree with most of it but could not seem to find any unity to fix it with all the duality issues of their reality. So our council leaders had determined it was time to step back, let humans learn the lessons from their own errors. Especially seeing how the new developments of particle weapons could affect our species. It was very dangerous and held negative consequences which humans could not understand yet but didn't seem to care. It appeared that a lot of damage to the planetary systems was being done but no matter how we warned them, they refused to hear us. So, it was time to let humans learn the old fashion way, by trial and error. We only wanted to make sure that we did not suffer with them.

We would step back in once it ran its course. In the meantime, we were to pull back to our dimension. My ship was currently cloaked, preparing to transport the last of our outpost members back to Terra Prime. Our security had just moved the device onboard. My woman, just about to give child birth, carried it onto the bridge. She was required to oversee the secure transport of the energy system first hand. This was the main power supply for our base. Once it was removed, the base would be closed. There would be no going back, at least not to a safe environment. With the power device removed, the cloaking device would disengage. Our Outpost would be observable. Governments would move in to secure the location. This was our cue to leave.

I was the last to board our craft. My job was to secure our cloaking device as all other technology had already been removed. All that would be left to show that we had ever even been here were buildings. While humans would be able to tell the construction was not normal, there would be nothing left to tip them off to exactly who we were and where we came from or where we went to. I placed the intricate device in a small chest of safe keeping. When I arrived on the bridge of my ship, I locked it in a secure compartment there. As I would spend my time in transit there, that was the best place for it. This technology was very powerful. It was my responsibility to make sure it returned to our dimension safely. This particular device was more than a cloaking device. It was an artificial intelligent apparatus designed to function on many levels including genetics, molecular reorganization, energy transformation and transmutation, or any other temporal needs. Basically, it could function as a device to cloak a city or it could act as a power generator not to mention its data storage and interface when needed. There wasn't much it couldn't do actually.

As I was one of the most powerful of my kind, supporting genetic anomalies and enhanced bio-technologies, I was the chosen protector of our species most powerful technology. My mate also was so augmented but in other ways, and her about to give birth to my first born. We were moving into the atmosphere preparing to make the journey to our home dimension. At the early stages no 3D structures could be nearby, we were required to move into a proper orbiting position before we initiated a temporal shift. Otherwise we would be torn apart by the surrounding matter.

Just as we were about to begin transit, our sensors picked up a hostile force entering Earth's orbit near us. We recognized it right off, an unauthorized slave trade alliance ship. While the ship appeared harmless enough, I should have known better than to take any chances with the technology we had on board. Instead, I ordered an intercept. I would capture their vessel to hold it for the proper authorities to ensure their failure. After all, we were Earth's guardians. At least that is how we viewed ourselves. As soon as we got within range of the vessel, it surprised us by opening fire on our ship. Generally no slave trade ship could possibly possess any type of weaponry that could harm our ship, there appeared to be a new sect of slavers. These had weapons we have never seen before and the damage was devastating.

In a moment's notice, we were going down, going down hard. Not only had they crippled our ship but all our computer controls were offline. Luckily our ship was designed to handle landings on planets with atmospheres. I felt we might land our craft and call for backup quickly enough. The only problem currently was our communications were also down. My orders were to get all systems back up asap. I took over manual controls to land the craft. We were going down. I took one last look at my woman. I smiled at her as she strapped herself in. No one was prepared for a crash landing. We were all caught off guard. Things were going in slow motion. I wondered if my woman and child would survive. Then I quickly assured myself that it could be no other way. And yet, we were going down. It was like a hazy dream suddenly and in slow motion, as if time had suddenly stretched beyond logic. But all I could think was, *we were going down.*

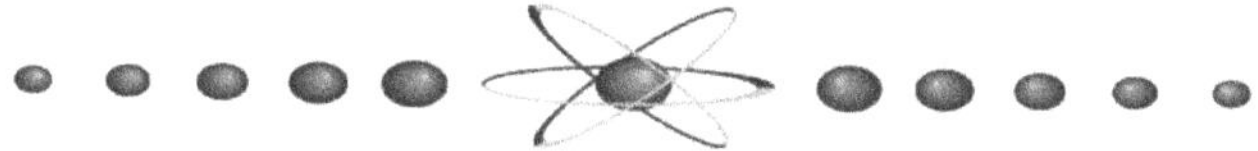

Some would say that humanity was highly advanced. Others might say that the story is only beginning, that the human species is a rough gemstone that will take many more years to polish. The greatest minds call our species barbaric, unrefined, and in need of major changes. Then there are the stories of extraordinary events, alien beings preying on humanity or watching over humanity. The stories are so varied and distorted that divisions of opinion keep it all blaring in a haze of muddied soup. No one seems to know the answers and when someone stands up to tell too much of realistic experiences, our government seems to make them disappear. But one thing is for certain, time continues its path of unrelenting focus. The tick tick tick of the clock.

So we find ourselves in the year 2024 with the american military advanced well beyond public capabilities in the field of genetic research. With most research institutions stagnating on the battlefield of competition, having pursued all the new techniques of gene therapy and enhancement drugs, the military secretly surged ahead. Public companies just did not have the imagination or the desire to pursue all avenues available. Military needs far exceed the normal loss of limb, Alzheimer, cancer or viruses popping up across the planet. Their needs were much greater.

Of course how could most companies know where to look with the government handling all the exotic situations across the planet? Dealing with aliens, mythological creatures, and some bordering on religious subjects: as you can imagine, over time a lot of information of unusual topics accumulated.

All hidden well away from the public's view. No one even considered the idea of discussing research on these extraordinary projects with publicly owned companies. It was just too controversial as it would have called into question so many base beliefs founded in religions and science, not to mention folklore and off world beings.

So quietly behind the scenes government projects were formed. A couple of research teams were created, specialty teams. The primary skills of these teams covered the sciences but each team member were heavily trained in military combat operations. Not only inside work but field work as well. They were required to be extremely talented in both areas. Usually you would think of a scientist as a geek or something but not these teams. They could blow your head off then perform the autopsy. This compartmentalized the whole operation. No need to have a team of scientists and a team of combat military personnel to guard and protect them. But more than that, the places they went required them to have both skills. It was that simple really.

The government kept them very busy. As more incidents of off-worlder missions arose, more and more specimen were being accumulated in laboratory studies exposing their diverse physiology. Soon the research took leaps and bounds in genetic mapping. That knowledge led to greater discoveries applied to human genetic manipulations.

The brightest minds were needed to head up these teams. None could compete with the scrappy blonde Dr. Keri Watts. Standing at a mere five feet tipping the scales with 135 lbs of ferocity, she could easily rip your guts out, stuff them into a beaker, and then spout out some geeky nerd data to make you eww and aww in your pants. She was simply amazing. Even wearing glasses she could mesmerize you with her cat like agility topped with her fluid movements of sexual enticement. A man's dream come to life. Too bad she was kept hidden away in the quiet corners of the labs most of the time. When off-world specimens were captured, they were delivered to her doorstep for handling.

Dr. Watts' main concern was turning off-world knowledge into on-world advances or as commonly noted, human genetic manipulations to improve our species. This was what it was all about. She did so love the missions off-base though. Leading a team into the thick of it wound her up. The excitement of it all combined with the need to make the changes she so desperately wanted to accomplish in science made her the ultimate candidate for the project. There was no mistaking that. Yet she basically lived on-base overseeing all the diverse life forms retrieved.

The other team leader excelled in field activities. With his twenty plus years running military ops across every terrain imaginable, none could compete with him. His tactical approach ensured a successful expedition no matter what the environment or encounter. His special operations team was the key to the needs of the project. Agent Timothy Ohm could quickly read the situation, scan the terrain, direct the interaction of team members in such a way that it was nearly impossible to fail. That's why he was in charge of the ground team. Timothy was a stern commander. He required absolute dedication to task.

So when he received the orders to take his team to south america, off he flew. Every time new orders arrived his heart would skip a beat, jar him just a little. The things he would see, the experiences were unimaginable. He couldn't even consider doing anything else with his life. That would be unacceptable to him, unthinkable. In his spare time he was always training. From martial arts to weapons specialities. He liked to take point on task out in the field. That way he was right in the middle of the action, always taking the most direct and dangerous role. He excelled in his craft. While officially his excuse for taking point was to insure the safety of his team, everyone knew he was addicted to the thrill. They all loved him for it though. He could do no wrong.

The new orders were clear. An off-world craft had crashed. Satellite images showed bodies. Not normal off-world bodies, green lizard humanoids, a first for Timothy. This was what he loved about his job. Today he would meet green lizard men. Well, maybe not meet, it would depend on if any were alive. No intel on that yet. Retrieve all specimens, alive or dead, preferably alive. It didn't matter though when it came down to it. Everything was studied under a microscope so thoroughly that not a single cell would escape once they were tagged, bagged and sent to Dr. Watts. And that was his job. Bringing live specimen was always the goal. Rarely did he fail there.

They brought the net cannons, the goo bombs, several hunt and grab spider robots and tons of exotic weapons and tools. Each one designed to capture or stop off-world creatures or other dimensional forms projected into our reality. A lot of velcro noises accompanied everyone during prep in transport. It would be dangerous in south america from the natural wildlife as it was. Timothy's favorite weapon was the stunner. He liked it best because it was a test of skills every time he used it. You had to literally touch the target with it knocking it out with a massive jolt of electricity. All he had to do was touch the target with it. Out like a light usually. There were a few occasions where that didn't happen. Just made it more interesting for Timothy though.

The teams had access to top secret aircraft. Speed was at their disposal. Super sonic velocity was nothing. They had stealth transports with ionic propulsion systems. It would only be a matter of minutes to arrival. A quick jaunt into the atmosphere with sudden acceleration horizontally found them right over their destination. That was always amazing to experience for the team. Hard to ever get used to moving somewhere that quickly.

"Time to lock and load", Timothy yelled to his team.

Timothy didn't know what to expect from this species as they had never encountered it before. He ordered electronic thought screeners activated long before they were anywhere near site. Just a precaution he explained. You could never be too safe in these situations. Sure didn't want to see teammates turning their weapons on each other as some creature took control of their mind. While it was rare, it could happen. That was one of the reasons they had developed non-lethal weaponry early on. While their weapons didn't disintegrate or destroy things in their path, they were very effective on biological targets. The pulse rifles were the closest thing to causing damage they possessed, yet their purpose in most cases was to keep things off them. It could be devastating to be pummeled by alien hominoids. Sometimes their strength was extreme. One blow could potentially kill.

As the team landed, Timothy set paths for each unit. Taking point he pushed right down the middle. The fastest and direct path. Allowing the other units enough time to move to the sides, he ordered his unit to advance. Smoke could be seen about fifty yards ahead when they slowed their pace. Caution became the primary concern when approaching unknowns. The insects played havoc on them but it would have been worse if not for their repellant. Spread to each side of Timothy were specialist in detecting jungle wildlife. It was imperative that no snake bites or nasty insects with venom would cause them issues. Nothing showed as they crept up on their target. Once the main part of the craft came into view they halted to take in their surroundings.

Timothy signaled the other teams with a push of a button that they had arrived. He received the silent signals on his wrist watch with low light flashes of red and blue. Each of the other teams were in place. Sending more coded messages to the other teams, he informed them to move forward slowly. Timothy could make out a few pieces of the vessel as it had partially broken up on landing. As they drew closer he could see that it was mostly intact except for part of the front section that had broken off. The craft had landed, skidding into a clearing caused by boulders. The boulders had obviously been the cause of most of the damage. You could see a few trees downed as it had come in at a slight angle.

Whoever was piloting had probably tried to land in the clearing not realizing the boulders which made the clearing would do so much damage to their craft. Bad break for them, good break for us. With all the smoke blowing through, it was hard to see the details. As they approached, one corpse was found sprawled across a boulder. It was a lizard humanoid alright. Long tail, scaly green skin, bone like protrusions on its back with slightly human facial features. It had been wearing some form of space suit which had shredded to fall away as it crawled onto this boulder before it died. After an intensive moment of excitement, it was definite, dead. A frothy white-green fluid had oozed out of its mouth. Numerous cuts where more green fluid showed the massive damage it sustained during the crash.

As a precaution, Timothy left one team member to guard the body. You never know, if it came back to life somehow, no sense in letting it surprise us from behind as we advanced on it's ship. Nearby were found two more bodies in similar states. If one were to guess, they would say the aliens weren't wearing space suits but only normal type of clothing like humans do. How else could you explain its fragile state. While one of the bodies was still in its clothes, the other two were bare of clothes, plainly showing it to be more decorative than necessary. One of the three corpses appeared to be female while the other two were male. No missing that as the female had blues and yellows as natural coloring on its head, down its back, ending with a flare of red at the tip of its tail. A sure sign of female coloring as attraction indicators which was normal to many reptiles.

Timothy ordered a thorough search around the craft before anyone took the next step to move inside it. He sent teams of two into the surrounding jungle to ensure there weren't any missing bodies adding orders to secure debris once a grid pattern search of a quarter mile was finished. They were very efficient. Less than thirty minutes to accomplish all goals. Soon they were back. In the meantime all three corpses were bagged up to be transported back to the base. By the time the search team had finished and returned, the transport was already back with backup personnel prepared to secure the ship. Larger transports were on the way to take the whole craft back to base to be studied for technological advances. The normal processes of such excursions.

It was time to move into the craft. They had no idea what would be found inside. There could be more creatures or any form of defense systems. Who knows, the ship could even end up self destructing or something if things went south. The next steps would be crucial in determining the outcome. The front of the craft had a large chunk of it missing on the bottom. While it was dark inside, there was a large hole in it. Obviously, that was where the bodies came from.

Excitement began to rise as they neared the dark hole. In preparation to move inside they had added a lighting rig to their gear. It would shine lights pretty much in all directions around them. This kept their hands free and provided lighting in dark places. Timothy moved in first. You never ask another to do something that you would not do yourself. Yet to prove that meant Timothy was generally the one to go first. But Timothy didn't mind in the least.

Stepping into the darkness, Timothy's light brought the control bridge into view. His team spread out to the sides as he hesitated to scope the scene out. It appeared to be vacant of life forms yet it was fully in disarray. Most of the systems were damaged with pieces scattered across the floor. Detecting no movements or life other than his team's, Timothy ordered his second in command James Burns to proceed deeper into the ship.

Timothy had full confidence in James, having spent years watching him develop his skills. James ordered his team into tactical exploration mode. They carefully proceeded out of the front section down a corridor leading off into the rest of the ship. The ship was a good hundred meters long and probably four times that in width, shaped like the wings of a bird. The front section was a good twenty meters wide at its deepest point having a five meter wide front area. It tapered wider as you would proceed towards the rear.

Timothy ordered his remaining team members to carefully evaluate this control bridge. Gather anything useful to shuttle to base as quickly as possible. They wouldn't have much time to do a quick search for other life forms or dangers before the main transport team arrived to haul off the craft. The usual business of hiding finds from competing governments and the public. Besides a few handheld devices, they found little to bag up. Once that was completed he took his team to join the other team in searching the ship.

After letting James know his team was moving up from behind, James directed them deeper into the middle section as he had split his team into two units branching one to each side of the craft. A single member was guarding the passageway directly to the rear of the craft. Timothy took his team past the guard who held his position after they passed. Nothing would be able to leave the craft without them knowing. The usual procedure for just these types of situations.

As Timothy's team moved further in, only finding storage areas with supplies which were mostly still in good shape having only been pummeled a bit from the crash. Luckily they were secured well in containers. No telling what would be found hidden in those. Timothy guessed it was food and medical supplies. After finding some personal quarters with some unusual devices or personal effects, the hallway suddenly ended, opening into a larger cargo bay.

They found what appeared to be cages with lots of animals indigenous to earth. Obviously the creatures were gathering samples from our planet. There were jungle cats, snakes, lots of diverse rodents, different types of deer or antelope, some reptiles, amphibians, birds, insects and many types of plants. They were definitely retrieving samples from our world. Timothy wondered where these beings came from. Another planet or possibly a different dimension. It was hard to say. Just as Timothy's team had finished securing the cargo area, James' team released an emergency call for reinforcements.

There appeared to be a live alien. It was putting up a hell of a fight. Timothy offered to bring his team to aid him. The other team had still not finished securing the west section so Timothy ordered them to continue while his team moved to the east section as reinforcements. As they arrived to assist James' team, they could plainly see the alien had taken down most of James' team members. It appeared the alien could direct heavy electric shocks into the soldiers from short distances.

The alien itself was drawing electricity from the air, storing it somehow in its own body. Off hand it looked like the fins on its back were the source of storage as you could see that area glow brighter when it discharged into its enemy. The alien was very fast and strong. As team members fired their pulse rifles the creature would dodge. A concussion grenade was thrown back into the team's vicinity showing the intelligence of it also. Timothy didn't hesitate. Charging right into the fray, pulling his stunner, even as he tagged the creature you just knew it was not going to work. Not only did it not work but the creature absorbed the electric charge from the stunner but sending it right back at Timothy taking him down.

The creature was standing over Timothy as if he were about to kill him when James dove from behind it to nail it right on the back of the head with his pulse rifle butt. A bit of blunt force to the back of the head sent the creature down, falling on top of Timothy. Of course Timothy didn't notice since he was unconscious. The way the two of them were stacked on the floor made for a funny scene. One of the younger team members took out his cell phone and snapped an image. Even on such a special team, humor played a major role in keeping up the spirits. Everyone knew that a copy of that photo would show up in Timothy's mailbox soon. Also, everyone knew not to tell who took the photo.

Now that this side of the craft was secure, half the team was sent to join the east team. It really wasn't necessary as within a few minutes of arriving, that side was proclaimed secure also. The live alien was sedated and cuffed. Nothing left to chance. It was kept under heavy guard until transportation could arrive to haul it. That would only be moments out.

Yet just after cuffing it, the creature had awakened to lash out at anyone near it. The sedation didn't seem to be effective at all. Another well placed rifle butt put an end to all concerns. Then more bonds were engaged on it leaving nothing to chance. James broke out the extreme sedatives at this point. We didn't want any more incidents with this alien. By the time we had the alien secure we noticed all his cuts and scratches had been healed. Obviously this creature was highly regenerative. Its strength was off the charts also. A prime specimen for sure. Off to the base we headed. A few more pieces of technology accompanied by a live specimen. What more could you ask for?

Passing off the specimen to Dr. Watts ended an exciting day for Timothy. Now it was time for Dr. Watts and her team to do their thing. Genetic samples were taken immediately. The full battery of tests were run on this new alien species.

Over time it began to work with Dr. Watt's team. It appeared to have a desire to assist them in understanding it. Soon the team learned to communicate with it. While its language was complex, Dr. Watts determined a basic understanding. From there forward, a lot of interaction and cooperation formed between it and Dr. Watt's team.

Timothy joined Dr. Watt's team as research began to progress on the devices captured along with the alien. After an accident in the lab occurred with the alien, Timothy gave it a nickname, Sparks. An unusual amount of static electricity had accumulated near Sparks. Unknown to Dr. Watts or Timothy, Sparks had unintentionally absorbed it, causing a discharge from it into the bars of Spark's cage. Sparks explained that the sudden surge of electricity caused him to lose control temporarily allowing it to discharge before he could stop it. The fins on his back would automatically absorb electricity right out of the air. After that procedures were put in place to keep those types of accidents from happening again.

Timothy could not convince Sparks to explain how the devices worked. Sparks only intimated that they were dangerous weapons. Timothy felt Sparks held a parental perspective concerning humans. As if he believed his race were somehow responsible for overseeing human development. Sparks wouldn't elaborate on the issues however, only explaining the weapons were too powerful for humans who would not utilize the knowledge properly. Even stating that humans would kill other humans with them and that would not be permitted. It didn't matter what or how

Timothy approached the subject of the weapons, Sparks refused to cooperate, leaving him empty handed. After a time Timothy decided to leave it to the reverse engineering unit. They would end up figuring out how they worked sooner or later.

Genetic Nightmare

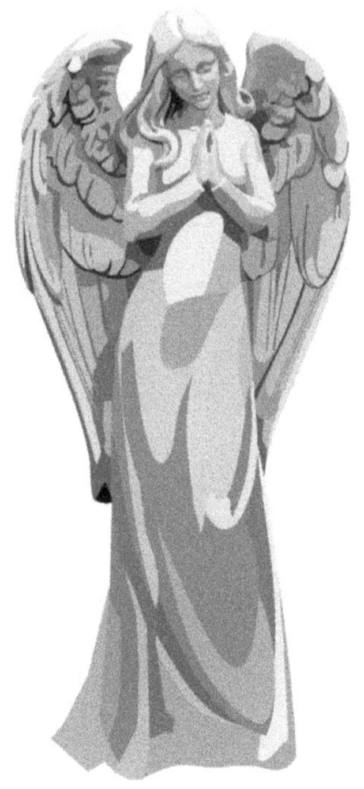

CHAPTER TWO

*The greatest value in life can be found in the interaction
with others...*

Pike

Santiago was beginning to worry for his wife Isabella. Their four year old son Samuel had recently died from malaria. He was Isabella's world. Every morning she would get him up, make him his favorite breakfast before allowing him to play. Santiago had purchase a horse ranch just outside of Lima Peru. While it was a good thirty miles from Lima, no one came around. They were a bit isolated down in a valley. Santiago had cleared the land, keeping the jungle at bay. He worked hard developing natural fencing for the horses close in to the house. Predators were a main concern of his after all.

He kept a number of larger dogs which he trained to stand guard at night. He loved the breed of Fila Brasileiro which was a rather large dog but could handle most anything that might come out of the jungle to bother the horses. Even the jaguar didn't stand a chance against them when they were trained properly. Some mornings he would get out of bed to find dead jungle cats from that night or large snakes looking for easy prey. His favorite dog was the biggest of the others which he named Valedor meaning Protector. Valedor weighed approximately 125 lbs, which was much more than the others. He was a brute. But Valedor was very loving and affectionate.

Santiago had raised him indoors, bonding with him. Valedor was like a son to him. So anytime Samuel went out to play, Valedor always trailed along. No matter what Samuel was doing, Valedor was always nearby keeping watch on the young toddler. Life was good. The horse breeding business was very profitable. Santiago had chosen to breed the Peruvian Paso horse. Thanks to its unique, inbom, four-beat lateral gait, the Peruvian horse is the smoothest riding horses in the world. Back in the seventeenth century, the Spanish brought them to Peru. They developed the Paso horse by blending the Barb, the Friesian, the Spanish Jennet, and the Andalusian breeds. In recent times the Paso had gained in value driving up the call for them. Santiago made a very good living. Fact is, most in Peru would say he is very rich.

That didn't comfort Santiago or Isabella when they lost their son Samuel though. They would gladly give up all their wealth just to have their son back. Isabella and Santiago were traveling over the mountains to visit family. Isabella's grieving had affected their lives so much that Santiago thought it was best to spend some time with Isabella's sister Mariana and her family. Santiago had his brother Matias watch his ranch while they were away. It was on their way over the mountain when the strange lights in the sky shot across their path to crash nearby. They had just rounded the mountain to find semi level roads. They were miles from anyone or anything.

A strange looking craft shot across in front of them. It happened so fast they weren't sure what they saw. It appeared they were seeing one side of a rather large airplane as the wing was plain to see. It came in so fast though, they weren't certain. They didn't hesitate to stop and help. Santiago was armed with a large machete and a pistol but he had Valedor with him also. Isabella followed close behind. Santiago noticed she wasn't paying much attention to her surroundings. That troubled him so he paid a lot of attention to any dangers that might bother her. They had only lost Samuel last week. Santiago was afraid that Isabella would become depressed. He had heard many stories of women who became so grieved that they never fully recovered. He decided to act quickly to help her. Family was the answer he was sure of it.

As they made their way into the jungle, he noticed smoke rising. He picked up the pace as he didn't want to be caught in a forest fire. That could be very bad. They could easily become trapped and die if that were to happen. He encouraged Isabella to pay attention and stay up with him. She began to move faster but Santiago noticed she still wasn't paying enough attention to her surroundings. He would have to watch out for both of them.

The crash site was just ahead. He slowed his pace not wanting to rush into a bad situation with fire spreading or something. He began to look around more just in case there were bodies or something thrown from the wreckage. As he approached the smoking aircraft it dawned on him that this was no ordinary craft. He had never seen anything like it. It was so big for one thing. He imagined it was a spy craft from america or something. He had heard many stories about those.

It was when he got right up beside it that he first glimpsed a body ahead through the smoke. Veldore began to bark as he stopped in front of them. Isabella wasn't paying any attention whatsoever. She was gliding through life without experiencing it. Santiago only hoped their trip was going to do the trick. Her sister could probably reach her but he wasn't having any success. He rushed toward the body as he could see it was moving. He stopped suddenly in his tracks, unable to move. Isabella stepped to his side, glancing ahead. Veldore stopped, sniffing the air. The alien form crawling on the ground took them completely by surprise. Santiago couldn't move, afraid that he might attract attention to himself or Isabella. Carefully reaching down to hold Veldore back he did a small jerk on his collar signaling him to stay put and keep quiet. Veldore obeyed without question.

While he had heard many rumors of aliens, he didn't recall any with green lizard like creatures. He glanced at the craft again. It began to sink in now, this was an alien craft and it had crashed in their jungle. He reached out his left hand to push it in front of Isabella wanting to back out of this nightmare. He took a slow step backwards trying to encourage Isabella to backup also but she was unresponsive. He looked to see why. She was staring at the alien on the ground and refused to move. He pushed on her but she reached out and pushed his arm aside as she moved forward. "Isabella, no!", he quietly yelled at her.

He looked to see if the alien had heard him as he reached for her arm to try to stop her. The alien had rolled over on its back. It was a female. He could tell because it was pregnant. It was looking at Isabella. Motioning for her to help it pointing at the baby bulging from its belly. Isabella ignored Santiago walking faster. She was definitely paying attention now. Santiago panicked, ran in front of Isabella. "Stop Isabella, this is an alien. It might hurt you or kill you.", he pleaded.

Isabella just looked into Santiago's eyes, begging him to move out of her way. He could tell she was not going to listen to him. She was always headstrong that way. Isabella went to the female alien, taking her hand in her own. Staring down into its eyes. The alien took Isabella's hand and placed it on her bulging stomach. You could see the look of desperation in its eyes. The intelligence in its eyes assured you of its intentions. It was dying and it wanted Isabella to save its baby. The alien made a slashing movement with its claw across its belly just below the baby. There was no denying what it wanted.

Isabella looked to Santiago with her pleading eyes. Her compassion was infectious. Taking a deep breath, Santiago stepped up to the female alien. Placing his hat into his hand he nodded his agreement. It was plain that the alien was in pain as she was bleeding from many wounds. Santiago pulled his hunting knife out, positioned himself to perform the surgery. He had done similar things in the past to cattle when he needed to save a calf as he grew up on his father's ranch. He suspected this would be no different other than the fact the alien would not survive. He felt sorry for it now.

Nodding his head to the alien to indicate he was about to proceed, the alien responded back. He could see the resignation in her face. She knew her time was ending. She was about to die. Santiago made the cut, watching the alien cringe in pain but not making any sound. He could see the baby moving inside her. Reaching in he pulled the baby alien out. He lovingly held it as he moved up to let the mother alien hold her baby before she died.

The alien cuddled its baby for a moment. Then as her color began to drain she looked at Isabella. She offered the baby to Isabella with pleading eyes. Isabella reluctantly took the child pulling it to her chest as she would any baby. The alien reached up one last time to caress her child snuggled in Isabella's arms. The female alien said something in a strange language. It was calm and assuring whatever she said. No one needed an interpreter to understand her intentions. Isabella nodded in agreement. Santiago knew what that meant. Then the female alien smiled. A look of comfort came over her face as she laid her head back releasing her last breath.

Santiago wiped his blade off, putting it away. He noticed a couple of other forms through the smoke when it eased a bit now and then. After checking on them, both dead, he was considering going into the alien craft. Checking for more dead there. Posting Veldore to guard Isabella, he carefully moved into the hole in the side of the craft. It was a mess. You could tell most of the controls were destroyed or not functioning. Santiago had to use a lighter he kept for emergencies. It was dark inside making it hard to see even with a lighter.

He stumbled over a small chest near where he entered. It was light but made of some type of metal. He couldn't see how to open it but he felt something moving around inside when he shook it. Then he heard a large sound outside. Looking out he could see Isabella looking upwards. Following her gaze he saw a strange craft circling their position over head. Hurriedly he jumped out of the craft, taking Isabella by the hand he encouraged her to make haste. They fled from the crash site, hoping no one had seen them there. Santiago wasn't sure if it was more aliens or humans coming to investigate. It didn't matter which one it was, they should not be anywhere near there when they came down. He told Isabella to head to their truck while he erased all sign of them having been there.

Veldore stayed with Isabella while Santiago removed their tracks in a hurried state of mind. He was thorough though, knowing a simple mistake could cost them their lives. Governments didn't like loose ends and aliens was a mystery to him. Either way, he wasn't about to let anyone know they had been there. Especially since he still carried this small chest he had recovered from inside the craft.

When he got back to the truck, Isabella was resting in the passenger's seat caring for the baby alien. Santiago asked her, "Isabella, what are we going to do with this alien baby?" She looked at him for a moment. Not saying a word she raised her chin taking on a stern and determined look as she stared straight ahead. There was no doubt what she intended. He knew the trip to her sister's was over. Yet he could see life in his wife's eyes again. The green alien seemed happy but to think about it all was very troubling to Santiago. He knew Isabella was suggesting that they would be raising this alien child as their own. Not only suggesting it but demanding it. It was out of his hands now. But he had his wife back.

While the situation was confusing for him, he was thankful that his wife was returning to normal. As for the alien baby, they would figure it out as they went. What more could he do?

Turning the truck around, he headed back for their ranch. He had his wife back but now he had a new son. What more could anyone ask for? Even if it was an alien son, he knew everything would be ok. Their ranch was way away from everyone else. They rarely got visitors as it was. As he drove home he decided to build on to their ranch house. An underground section would be required now. That would ensure their child's safety. If the intelligence of the female alien was any indicator of what this child would be like, they would have a handful he knew.

Life had a way of taking care of things. Even if it handed you an alien baby in the process. Santiago was only grateful that all was well in the world. He determined to make it all work out, no matter what. He smiled as he heard Isabella begin to hum a lullaby to the baby. He said to Isabella, "We'll call him Pike.". She only nodded her head in agreement. Life was good again.

Genetic Nightmare

CHAPTER THREE

The choices *we* make today have consequences
tomorrow...

Total Shutdown

Dr. Watts developed a formula from Sparks' genetic samples designed to heal human tissue at an accelerated pace. She estimated extremely fast tissue growth would be the result. Just as the testing protocols were developed for further data accumulation, the teams were shut down by the government. No one knew the reasoning, only that it was over. Some government agency stepped in, shut everything down, sent everyone packing with non-disclosure orders threatening death or prison if any leaks developed. They loaded up all the aliens, including Sparks, hauling them off. The usual government secrecy issues.

Behind the scenes Timothy and Dr. Watts had developed a secret relationship. Knowing it was forbidden, they had kept it quiet. Now with the program shut down, they moved into an apartment together. No reason to hide it any longer. After a while some of the old team members decided to have a get together. Timothy and Keri along with a few of Timothy's team, namely Aidra, Coyote, James, and Drake, met up to celebrate the old times of glory. After dinner and drinks, Keri and Aidra decided to go shopping.

Timothy and James sat down for extra drinks needing to discuss their civilian lives and what kind of work they might pursue together. James kept encouraging Timothy to join him in returning to special ops with the military. Timothy didn't want to spend that much time away from his new love Keri so he was avoiding that direction. A compromise was negotiated, private security work was the answer. They would start their own company beginning next week. Timothy had it all figured out. Some of his old associates would help him get things going. They had already contacted Timothy a few times but Timothy had been avoiding following through until he could sit down with James. He didn't want to do anything like that without his right hand man.

It was settled. After a bit more conversation and another round of drinks, Timothy headed home. One stop on the way. He was planning on surprising Keri later tonight. His cousin was going to meet him at their jewelry shop so he could pick up a nice engagement ring. Tonight he was going to pop the question. He didn't want to wait another day. Now that their future plans were settled, he felt good about everything. The most beautiful and smartest woman he has ever known would be his soon. Today would be the greatest day of his life. Smiling, he headed downtown.

Just like any good plans, everything can come to a sudden halt. Who can foresee events that are approaching at breakneck speed to end all those well laid agendas. Even relationships can suddenly evaporate right before one's eyes. On top of all those, the best intentions can backfire on you just as quickly as a lightning strike. So it was as Timothy arrived home before Keri and Aidra had finished shopping. Not by much but just enough to save Keri's life.

Aidra dropped Keri by her apartment. Of course Keri asked her to come up for a while. As Keri opened the door leading into their apartment section, an oppressive feeling settled in on her. One of those moments where you know something has taken place without knowing what it could possibly be. A panic set in as she rushed upstairs the dread of the moment washing over her. Women's intuition can be strong when every moment can count.

As she rushed to her apartment doorway, she noticed the door wide open. Fear gripped her right then. What would she see? Was there a burglar inside right now? Had their apartment been stripped of possessions? She froze, fearing the unknown. Pulling out her cell phone she called Timothy. As she heard Timothy's phone ring in her ear, she could also hear another phone echoing from within her apartment. It matched the noise in her ear, even when she canceled the call suddenly. The other phone stopped ringing.

So Timothy was already here. He probably just left the door open or something. She remembered he was going to have extra drinks with James. He might be passed out on the couch or something. The fear drained as she realized just how silly she was being. She had been ignoring Aidra's questions about what was up. She felt stupid now, giving Aidra a look of apology for her actions. "Sorry, I had a panic attack for some reason.", she explained to Aidra.

"Forget about it girl.", Aidra replied.

They proceeded to the open doorway expecting to see Timothy flopped down on the couch. As Keri stepped into the doorway with a smile on her face, her sudden stop caused Aidra to walk into her.

"Girl, you gotta warn me before you stop like that.", said Aidra.

It was all the blood on the floor that froze Keri so suddenly. That combined with the smell of gunpowder. On the floor were pieces of Timothy. His arm was several feet from his body with a bloody outline on the wall where it had rebounded before settling against the side of the couch.

Timothy was still spurting blood from his armless shoulder and chest wound. Obviously a shotgun blast. Timothy was convulsing but still breathing. His leg was also missing having taken another blast down low on one side. She could see it partially sticking out from behind the islander which led into the kitchen. Luckily for Timothy, Keri's medical training kicked in as she rushed to get a couple of sheets and some towels. In her mind she knew that Timothy would not survive if she called an ambulance or even rushed him to the hospital. No facility in the world could save Timothy.

Then she remembered her last project. She recalled the backup container hidden in the spare refrigerator where she had placed it for safety. The formula for accelerated healing at the lab. It had only been tried on a three legged rat named Nil. It had been a success with Nil, growing back his lost limb. Even if the limb was green, it still grew back. Her research had been cut short by the closure of their project but she still had access to her old lab. Screaming at Aidra to help her get Timothy loaded in her van, they proceeded to scramble to the lab.

Contacting her lab assistance Dr. Hope Songe, she agreed to meet her at the lab. As they wheeled Timothy into the lab his breathing became so shallow that Keri wondered if they were in time.

Kicking the evaluation system on they placed Timothy into the large tank as Keri rushed to retrieve the formula from the back room. In a matter of seconds she had injected Timothy as a last resort to save him. Moments later his breathing leveled out, his vitals became normal. All she could do was cross her fingers.

Keri and Dr. Songe spent the next few months monitoring Timothy in his medically induced coma as they continued his treatment with Keri's serum. His arm and leg were slowly regenerating. Of course they were green. Keri was having trouble determining why. There was no reason for it that she could detect. Everything appeared as normal down to the smallest details. Well, Timothy would just have to get used to the idea of a green arm and leg. Keri didn't mind. Just as long as she didn't lose him, she was happily content.

It was during that first week that Keri had doubted her choice. Crying herself to sleep each night she questioned her own sanity. But she knew if not for this, Timothy would already be dead. There was no doubt about that. Keri found herself staring at the ring she had found on the floor beside Timothy. It was still in the box. She saw the receipt from Timothy's cousin's jewelry store. A bit over five thousand dollars. Timothy had gone all out. It read, engagement ring, right on the receipt. Timothy was going to ask her to marry him. She knew her answer. There could never be another answer. He had captured her heart a long time ago.

It was during a late night movie at home. There was a part that was very sad making Keri cry. She was snuggled up against Timothy. She didn't think Timothy was paying any attention to the movie. She didn't really care as long as he was there with her. That was what really mattered most to her. As she began to cry from the movie, she looked up into Timothy's eyes. She could see a tear forming at the edge of his eyes. Then he turned away as if he wasn't watching. Seeing his tender side made her fall in love with him. There was no going back after that. Her heart belonged to no other. There was nothing she could do. She was hopelessly lost in his shadow. She refused to say she loved him until he said it first. She didn't want to jinx it.

But now, here they were in the lab. Timothy had nearly died. The alien serum was working. But no one could know about this though. Dr. Songe agreed. Until more research could be done they would have to be very careful and keep their mouths shut. Luckily, no one even bothered to check on the lab in all those months. Then things went off the charts.

It happened late in the evening after Keri and Dr. Songe had gone home for the day. Unknown to Keri or Dr. Songe, the drugs which had kept Timothy sedated were no longer effective as Timothy's regeneration had accelerated.

Timothy woke from his drug induced coma. Finding himself in a regeneration tank confused him. As he pulled himself from the coffin sized machine, his gaze fell on his green arm. The frenzy of uncontrollable panic gripped his very soul, his green leg caught his eye pushing him over the edge.

Unforeseen by Keri and Dr. Songe was the knowledge that adrenaline would mutate the regeneration formula which had saved Timothy's life so recently. In Timothy's accelerated state of regeneration, when his body produced adrenaline from his shock, the mutations came near instantly. Black veins began to bulge across his body. It was only a matter of moments before Timothy's whole body changed. With his mutations came a raging state of mind finding Timothy tearing through steel and brick alike as he made his way directly out of the facility. His new form made him unrecognizable as his eyes grew larger into almond shapes. His skin turned green while his hair fell out. His once human shaped skull rounded into an alien shape. Pushing out behind him was a scaled reptilian tail measuring a good five feet in length. Bone like fins pushed out of his back and shoulder blades to begin absorbing electricity from all around him causing small electric discharges between them. In his blind rage he barely noticed as sharp claws protruded out of his once human fingertips tearing through steel, wood and masonry shredding everything in his path.

Dark shadows calling him deep into the city to scream his unearthly sounds at the moon in anger and confusion. Calm thoughts far from his scattered mind as fangs pushed from his mouth. His once beautiful eyes taking on strange alien shapes as blue light glinted from them. Not remembering who he was or what happened to him was probably the only blessing in those moments of misshapen screams of agony. Who was he, where did he come from, why did he look like he did? Knowing it wasn't normal amplifying his tortured thoughts driving him into a berserker rage.

Keri had just gotten back to her apartment when her phone went off. The alarm at the lab had been triggered. Dr. Songe would also have been notified. She rushed back to the lab as quickly as she could without getting a speeding ticket. She knew that the police could not be contacted. She had one of Timothy's pistols in the glovebox. Just in case something went wrong, she would be prepared to take quick measures.

She did not expect the view that rolled out in front of her as she pulled up to the front of the building. On one side of the building was a rather large hole. It looked like something had just pushed through from the inside. Dr. Songe arrived just as

Keri was getting out of her car. They both walked together towards the hole. Keri had the pistol in her hand, ready for action if needed. This was very strange. Why would there be a hole in the wall? Who could have done this? What the hell was going on? All those thoughts were running through Keri's mind.

They didn't need a key to enter the lab tonight. After a cursory search of the buildings, they found that Timothy was gone. All the damage led straight to his room where he was being treated. They headed to the security office to view the security footage. It didn't take long before they knew exactly what happened. After a short period of discussions, they both began to suspect that the reaction of the mutations must have been triggered by Timothy's panic. Keri doesn't hesitate, she calls James Burns. Asking James to put together a team to help find Timothy. James reaches out to several of their old team members.

Aidra Agaro, Coyote Wilde and Drake Smith. Aidra, in her early thirties, was a specialist in fauna, psychology, and transportation repair but she was a main figure on Timothy's old team and one that could be trusted. Trust was key to their goal. Aidra had dark hair and that dark tan which attracted a lot of men to hit on her. The dark mysterious woman with the south american accent. Coyote was a specialist in weapons, gadgets and used to be a medic in the military. His southern accent made him easy to talk to when combined with his older chiseled features being in his forties. Drake was in his early twenties. One of those young stud muffins with looks to kill. The young girls would always flock to him when he would go dancing or clubbing. His specialties were hand to hand combat, weapons master and he was a communications specialist. Not to mention they each had expanded training in the sciences.

Their first order of business was to plan a search grid across the city. Then follow a plan of action which James put together to find Timothy. It was going to be an all nighter and more probably. But that was what friends were for. No man left behind motto was first and foremost on their minds. After watching the security footage though, they decided to retrieve some speciality weapons along the non-lethal description. This was not going to be a piece of cake. They knew Timothy was not himself and might attempt to kill them. Seek and capture, their specialty. If anyone could find Timothy and bring him back alive, it was them.

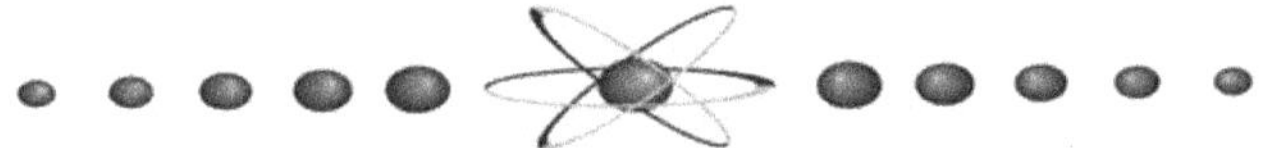

Timothy took to the shadows as he sought out a clothes store on a side street. He couldn't remember who he was or what he was, only that he should not be what he was. It was all foreign to him. As he searched in the dark, which was nearly bright as day to his new senses, he caught sight of himself in a mirror. The form he saw looked familiar. Yet he couldn't remember where he had seen it before. It was very frustrating to him. Very confusing overall. Yet he was determined to make due. He was always a survivor after all. This was just another day now as he calmed down. He would figure this out, whatever it all meant.

As he looked into his own eyes, he knew what looked back was not supposed to be him. Something had happened to him, but he didn't know what. Flashes of images from past events shot through his mind. They were all jumbled and made no sense to him. His instincts said to hide his body from view. He was listening to that inner voice now. What else could he do? At least that is what he told himself. Timothy found some pants, a shirt and trench coat to cover his features. Grabbing a hat to finish his look. As he gazed in the mirror one final time, he felt pleased with his choices. *Not so bad,* he thought. Almost human looking. He knew he could pass for a human at night anyways.

That would have to do. He began to understand those basic ideas of human and non-human.

Knowing he was human yet not understanding why he didn't look like one. That was his major thoughts just then. He fought to control his rage. He couldn't think clearly when he raged like that. He had to keep his mind calm. It was a battle as something deep within him was pushing to express itself. Yet his recent rash of anger had blinded him to everything. He wasn't even sure he remembered where he was at earlier in the evening. Some kind of facility but when he fled in a full blown rage, his mind fogged up. For now he would find a hiding place to hole up so that he could think things through and figure this out.

Just as he was about to leave the clothes store his sharp senses kicked in. He could hear a man threatening a couple in the back alleyway. "Give me your money.", he heard someone say. Rushing to the back entrance he stared out into the darkness. At least it was dark when considering human's vision. But Timothy could plainly see a large brute of a man holding a knife to the man's throat as the young couple were backed up against a dumpster in the alley. Another with a gun stood nearby pointing it at the woman.

"Just give me your purse lady.", the thug with the knife blurts out to the woman.

As she hands the one with the gun her purse she catches a glimpse of Timothy as he stealthily walks up behind the one with the knife.

At first the lady seemed reassured but as Timothy comes into view from the light at the back door across from them, she screams. Backing away from the thugs she runs into the dumpster. As she screams the two would be muggers turn to see Timothy also. Everything goes slow motion as they both look to the other to see what they will do.

Fight or flee, appears to be the questioning looks exchanged.

Timothy is so fast that they don't have a chance to make up their minds. The one with the gun finds himself heaved into the air as Timothy launches him into the other sending them both crashing into the wall a good six feet away. Barely getting out a scream, the two would be muggers bounce off the wall, landing in a heap on the ground unconscious. The man and woman fall to the ground cringing in horror as Timothy looks down on them. Seeing the fear in their eyes, Timothy flees into the cold dank darkness.

Yet it is this very human reaction to criminal behavior that leads the team to hear about it on the news as the police are called to investigate. All the team members are called to this location to begin a sweep from that point hoping to find Timothy before he is spotted by anyone else.

Genetic Nightmare

CHAPTER FOUR

Family is more important than anything, even the Law...

Pike Escapes

Santiago had spent a small fortune the last month building his new underground hideaway. Having to hire a construction company with hundreds of workers was a large investment. What else could he do? He needed the underground extension of the house done as soon as possible. Isabella was nearly back to normal. Spending all of her time caring for her new son kept her distracted. She barely said a word but the light in her eyes was back. That meant more to Santiago than anything. Even before they had lost their son, Isabella was not one for words.

The excavation was coming along very well. He decided to expand well beyond the scope of their old ranch house. Isabella stayed upstairs most of the time so there were no incidents with Pike. They would have a secure area underground to raise Pike away from the prying eyes of the world. He expanded the kennels also. Brought in more dogs. Santiago decided to add a herd of cows as Pike seemed to have a taste for meat. Yes, even as a newborn he ignored most attempts to feed him except for meat. Seemed logical though seeing as he appeared to be of reptilian origins.

The little tike was growing in leaps and bounds. In one month he had already grown a full six inches. Isabella was having trouble keeping him occupied upstairs. Santiago insisted they finish up the construction by the end of the week no matter how many workers it took, money was not an issue. Of course the construction company took advantage of his words by sending in a dozen more employees. Santiago was pretty sure they just pulled them off the street. Several looked like they didn't know what they were doing at all. It was no matter, as long as the work was finished soon.

They couldn't have anyone seeing Pike. Santiago knew where that would lead. Authorities showing up on his doorstep dragging Pike away.

No doubt about that. Or worse, they might decide to take matters into their own hands. Either way he knew word would spread very quickly. Then there would be nowhere to hide. He also posted warning signs about trespassers. Posted his property as private with trespassers to be shot on site.

Then the day before construction was to be finished, Pike disappeared in the middle of the night. He was a playful one and was quickly learning about his surroundings. Walking was no problem for him since the second day after he was born. Every time he would attempt to wander away from Isabella, she had scolded him. It was working very well at first. But the last few days his attempts to follow Isabella out the upstairs bedroom door were becoming harder for her to deal with. Her scoldings weren't as effective anymore.

Even her sternest voice but brought a smile from him now. So the last morning of the construction found him gone as Santiago and

Isabella woke. He was just gone. Santiago noticed first, scouring the room's corners and crevices for him. He was no longer in their room. Isabella woke as he checked beneath the bed. You could see the panic in her eyes, his too.

Santiago knew there would be many workers outside already. He wasn't sure what would happen next but he had to do something. Grabbing a laundry bag he headed out. Calling Valedor, letting him sniff Pike's toy, he ordered him to find Pike. Off they went. Valedor made his way through the house, into the kitchen. Santiago saw the meat wrappers from the fridge as Pike had obviously eaten his fill first thing. Santiago followed Valedor from room to room as he followed his scent.

He could see more and more workers through the windows going about their business gathering up loose material or finishing aspects of the construction. No screams or yells yet. Every hair on his arms was standing tall just then. Not sure what to do if anyone saw Pike. He only knew he was going to get him in the bag one way or another and hopefully before anyone sees him. After going all through the house Valedor indicated the trail ended at an open window. Pike had obviously opened it.

That little one was just too smart for his own good, Santiago thought.

He took Valedor outside, around to the window to pick up his trail. Spotting his tracks caused Santiago to panic a little. If any of the workers noticed the strange tracks, that could become a large problem. A two legged reptilian would not set right with any experienced tracker. As he followed the tracks he concentrated on dragging his own feet over them. Get rid of them before someone spotted them. He was about halfway across his yard when the construction foreman called to him. Turning he could see

Roberto walking at a fast pace towards him. He went to meet him to keep him away from Pike's tracks.

"Hola Santiago.", said Roberto. Santiago greeted Roberto, "Hola Roberto. What's up?" Roberto said, "We should be finished in the next few hours. We'll have everything packed up and out soon. I thought you would want to know." Santiago replied, "Thanks for letting me know Roberto. The quicker the better, we have a lot of things to do and Isabella is getting impatient to get started."

Roberto nodded his head, said his good day, turned away to go back to work. Santiago took a deep breath, headed back to continue his work of removing Pike's tracks. Santiago was removing all traces of Pike's tracks. They continued across the yard disappearing into the jungle about a hundred yards out. Now Santiago was growing concerned for Pike's welfare. There were all kinds of predators out there. Pike was just a little thing, barely two feet tall now.

He let Valedor take the lead hoping he could keep the scent. Another fifty yards or so in, Valedor lost his scent. Pike had run up a tree. Santiago noticed jungle cat prints around the tree. So Pike was smart enough to avoid it by running up the large tree. You could tell the large cat had gone round and round the tree. You could see where the cat had tried to climb into the tree going after Pike. Santiago knew Pike would be safe for the most part in the trees. Hope was returning to his mind. The cat tracks headed back off into the jungle. Santiago wondered if the cat was following Pike from below, keeping an eye on his anticipated dinner.

With Valedor leading the way, Santiago followed the cat's tracks. It was rough going. Plus Santiago had to keep an eye out for the normal jungle predators. It can be very dangerous in the jungle he knew. He began to notice pieces of fruit which grow in the higher levels which were now on the ground with the cat's tracks veering around them. Obviously the cat was following Pike and he was taunting the cat by throwing fruit at it. Santiago estimated the tracks were from late the previous evening. That meant that Pike had been out all night long.

After another couple of hundred yards or so Santiago noticed some new tracks join the cats. On closer examination he decided it was a human. Probably a hunter tracking the large cat. Their hides were worth a lot so many would hunt them to earn a living. It was a bit surprising that anyone would come this close to his ranch though. Now he was afraid for Pike. Luckily he could tell the new tracks were very fresh. Probably made in the last hour or two. He picked up his pace hoping to catch up to the trio before the hunter had a chance to find Pike.

He was afraid to go into a full run but he settled for a trot. He should have grabbed one of his own guns but with his hurried departure attempting to find Pike, he had neglected his own personal rules. Never go into the jungle without a good weapon. He hoped that Isabella would be patient as he had been gone for a couple of hours now. The tracks led further and further into the jungle. He was several miles from his ranch now but he felt like he was gaining on the hunter. He refused to stop and rest yet and luckily he hadn't come across any large predators. A few snakes and masses of insects but nothing he couldn't handle.

Another hour and he felt like the hunter's tracks were being made as quickly as he spotted them. Then he could hear something just ahead. He began to catch glimpses of what looked like a person. The cat's tracks were a little fresher but Santiago could still tell they had been made in the middle of the night or at least several hours before he had found the first sets at the tree that Pike had climbed. He began to wonder if Pike was running away. His trail was leading Santiago to the southwest, away from the ranch.

Checking the sun, Santiago realized that the path had circled to the south now. Maybe Pike was turning back at this point. It wasn't as if he had suddenly changed directions, it had happened over a period of time. Hopefully Pike knew which way he was going. Signaling Valedor to keep quiet he tried to close the distance between him and the hunter without alerting the hunter to his presence. He knew a good hunter would be checking his back trail regularly, so this hunter couldn't be a professional. That filled him with hope but still, how would he convince a hunter not to go after the cat.

Santiago still hadn't worked out that concept yet. He was making progress though. Slowly he was overtaking the hunter. Less than a hundred yards separated them now. He got flashes of a rifle and machete. This encounter could become very dangerous quickly if the hunter felt threatened by him.

With the thick jungle he couldn't tell much more about them. Just as Santiago was about 25 yards from the hunter, the hunter stopped dead in his tracks. He was leveling his rifle for a shot. Santiago rushed up behind the hunter as quietly as he could. A full grown man. He wondered if he should sic Valedor on him but that would definitely turn the hunter against him and probably cost Valedor his life. Not a good choice so he held his breath the last few yards trying to get right up on the hunter before he knew Santiago was even there.

It felt like it was taking an eternity to reach him. As Santiago came up behind the hunter he noticed the large black jungle cat about fifty yards further in. It was at the bottom of a tree standing on two legs while it watched something in the trees. Pike probably. Then Santiago noticed the hunter raise his rifle up, aiming it into the trees. It had a scope on it.

Oh no, Santiago thought. He's going to see Pike.

Santiago panicked, grabbing the hunter's rifle as he ran up behind him. The hunter had heard him coming as he was right behind him. Turning, the hunter had brought the rifle around but Santiago grabbed the side of the barrel as it was swinging around. Santiago was facing a masked hunter. Even though he was not a professional hunter, he appeared to be trained with weapons as he swung the rifle butt around hitting Santiago in the temple. Lights went off in Santiago's head, followed by the ground suddenly rushing up to greet him just as everything went black.

His last thought before the darkness closed in was his own voice scolding himself for not bringing a weapon.

Genetic Nightmare

CHAPTER FIVE

The decisions of yesterday turn into the
consequences of today...

Tracking Timothy

Keri decided it was time to fill James in on Timothy's incident and then transformation. Just as she was getting deep into the explanation the tv began to blare the emergency downtown, a broadcast on the 10 o'clock local news channel. James began to scramble the team to head to the location downtown. Keri follows James outside to join them as they load into the black suv. Speeding downtown, James barks orders to the others as they prepare to track Timothy. Keri, carrying a new device, fills James in on its capabilities. Tuned to Timothy's unique abilities manipulating electricity, by getting close enough to his' location she feels he can be tracked.

Arriving at the scene, cordoned off with police tape, James heads right through the officers towards the alleyway. Flashing his badge while motioning Keri over, James fills the officer in on their needs. Once Keri arrives the officer brings them up to date on the incident. It appeared that a couple were attacked in the back alley by two thugs. While being accosted by the muggers a large creature came out of the shadows, attacked the two muggers, knocking them out, then ran off into the shadows. Upon further investigation of the area, it appeared that the creature had robbed one of the clothes stores there and upon exiting from that building had run right into the scene in the alleyway. The store owner had reported a few clothing items missing but nothing more. A very strange incident by any means. The officer shakes his head with a look of disbelief as if he didn't understand any of it himself.

After the officer finished his story, Keri and James head further into the dark rainy alley.

"James, mind telling me how you got us past that cop?"

James leans in and whispers, "I managed to keep a couple of our government badges after we were shut down from the field days. So how does your little doohickey thing work anyways?"

Keri glanced at the device in her hand, having forgotten it as she left the suv.

"Well, this little antenna on top will triangulate Timothy's location by disturbances in the atmospheric electric fields. Since Timothy will be drawing energy from the air all around him to store it in his body, this little puppy will register those changes of energy. But we have to be within a mile or so of his location before it can function properly. Otherwise it only catches localized disturbances which aren't strong enough to set it off."

With a thoughtful look on his face, James asks Keri, "So, Timothy was dying fast and the only way to save him was to inject him with your serum?"

A tear began to form at the corner of Keri's eyes, "I had to James, he would have died right then. You know I love him. He was going to ask me to marry him."

James looked away. A stern look showed on his features but his eyes soften as he looks down. He knows that he would have done the same thing if he were in Keri's shoes. Timothy was like family to him, like a big brother.

James slips his arm around her to comfort her as they walk further in, "It's ok Keri, I would have done the same thing. Let's just get him home before someone kills him."

Keri sniffed away her emotions, wiping the tears from her eyes. After reviewing the scene in the alley, they headed back to the suvs where the others patiently waited. Jumping into the lead suv James ordered them to head out of town in the direction Keri pointed as she watched her gizmo.

Keri spoke up, "It appears he's about a mile from here, due west. The signal shows him moving further away at a decent pace. If we hurry we should catch up to him quickly."

James nodded. Coyote was driving, he sped up, heading west as Keri instructed. They were making good time. After about a half mile, Keri indicated that Timothy has stopped moving. The signal appeared to weaken as if he had moved inside of a building or something.

Keri said, "He stopped moving and the signal is weaker. Looks like he moved inside. But there aren't any buildings out there that i'm aware of. He must have gone underground or into a cave or something. That's the only thing that could account for my readings.

James explained, "That will make it easier to capture him then. He will be cornered."

Keri nodded in agreement.

James began barking orders through the communication system, making sure the mercenary team in the other suv followed his orders, "No lethals. Our target is a tall green lizard looking creature. We have to take him alive. Absolutely no lethals."

After turning the comm off he faced his team members in his suv, "The problem is, it's Timothy Ohm. Recently his life was in danger and under emergency conditions, a serum was given to him that saved his life. Unknown to Dr. Watts there were possible side effects. He mutated. At the time it was the only way to save his life. When Timothy mutated, he broke out of his confinement. We need to get him home safe and sound before some lame brain jock with a gun kills him or Timothy kills someone. We can't allow the other team members to find out this information. So here we are. Any questions?"

Aidra looked to James, then to Coyote. Coyote just shook his head with a sympathetic look. Aidra took on a determined look. It was obvious she was sympathetic to Keri's actions.

After giving everyone a moment, James continued, "Ok, we'll use close quarters engagement techniques, the usual formation. Keep your eyes peeled, your ears open, watch your man's back, and lets do this."

Everyone spouted out in unison, "Sharp and steady, let's do it!"

James smiled as he remembered the good ole days. His team was still tight. They were family. Each depending on the others to watch their backs in tight spots. He could tell they missed the action together. They were a well oiled team. You can't buy that with money. It takes sweat, blood and lots of time. It made him proud to know these brave souls. He called and they came running. Everyone knew their role. James only hoped that no one got hurt or killed by Timothy. He knew they wouldn't intentionally harm Timothy. This would not be easy and they knew the risks. But here they were ready to rock and roll. James felt a tear forming. He looked away from the others to brush his face against the side of his arm casually so they wouldn't notice.

Timothy was badly shaken. It was difficult to think straight. His memories were all garbled up, running over each other and fuzzy. How did this happen to him? His emotions were hard to handle also. They were spiking out of control at times and he would have to rein them in as best he could. He wanted to keep a cool head but was having a rough time of it. He continued to travel into the woods seeking a hiding place so that he could try to work things out in his mind. He slowed his pace now that he was clear of the city. No houses around these parts, just rugged outdoors, hills and gullies, creeks and ponds. Ahead he could see some higher ground. Maybe a cave or something would do?

He noticed just how touchy he was feeling to the weather. Lots of fluctuations along his back. He could feel energy building there. It felt natural to him. He noticed that if he thought about the electricity being pulled into his back that it would ready itself. Almost like it waited for him to instruct it what to do. He tested it on a tree as he was walking. A bright flash blinded him as lightning shot off his fins over his shoulders from behind. The damage was instantaneous. It ripped right through the tree causing a fire to start. It pushed back on him rather brusquely too. He had to catch his balance as he felt himself being pushed backwards when it went off.

Just about then he spotted a cave entrance ahead. He headed that way. Memories of his past began flooding into his mind. Pictures of a house warming party with gifts. A beautiful woman was beside him. Lots of friends were there shaking his hand and hugging the woman. He seemed to recall a name for the woman, Keri. Yea that was it, Keri. But who was she? What was she doing with him? What happened to her? The memories only angered Timothy more. You could hear him growl out loud. After Timothy searched a small cave, about ten feet deep and a few feet wide, finding it empty, Timothy sat down to think. Pushing his emotions to the side he tried to bring the pieces together. He remembered waking up in a building and breaking out of it. It was all a hazy fog of anger and fear combined. He wasn't even sure if he could find his way back. It happened so fast. Once he was out of that building, he ran and ran and ran. It was all a blur. Now he was alone and confused. He had to clear his head and think. Figure this out. He knew if he gave it enough time he could gather his wits, gradually work his way through his memories. They continued to shoot in and out of his head but he could tell they were settling down.

He suddenly felt a fluctuation in the energy around him. From his recent run through the city, he knew it was cars or trucks that felt like that. Someone was coming. More than one vehicle, he surmised from the multiple tugs on his back. He jumped to his feet, running outside. Looking down the sloped hill, he could make out several trucks headed his way. He could sense a number of people in them. They must be looking for him. He would stop them. Mustering all the energy he could from the air, Timothy began to draw in an astounding amount of electricity. He felt much stronger. He continued to draw more and more energy as he waited for them to get a bit closer to his location. He would do what felt natural. Somehow he knew this would stop them.

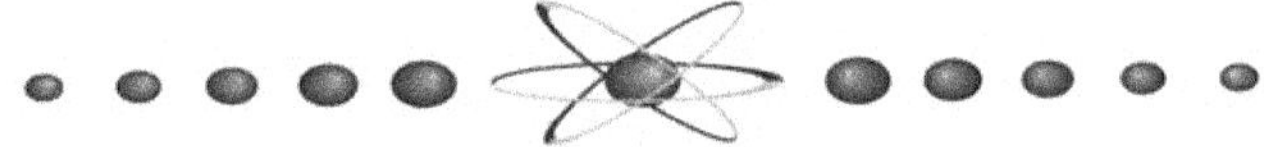

General Halstrom began barking orders, "The target is near our location. We don't know the capabilities of it except for its control over electricity. Coms are dark along with any other electrical devices. Team 1, I want you too spread out from both sides. Team 2 will head from the back. I cannot emphasize how important it is to capture the target alive. Team 1, you are armed with heavy sedatives. Team 2, you are armed with live ammunition, your job will be to make the target push forward with limited fire towards the ground but not at the target. You are to box it in as

Team 1 pushes in to sedate it. Once it's surrounded, shoot off a flare to give your location. Here are the last coordinates. There is a cave about 1 klick from here. We will search there first. I want whatever it is found and captured alive if possible!

The two groups of mercenaries respond in unison, "SIR! YES SIR!" It was just at that moment that lightning seemed to shoot across the landscape, halting all the trucks. Smoke began to pour from all their electronic devices, including from under the hoods of the trucks. General Halstrom jumped from his truck ordering his teams into action. A bank of fog had suddenly moved into the area, making it difficult to see more than a few feet. Halstrom smiled, knowing he was about to lay his hands on the first alien-human hybrid. A creature with superhuman abilities. His dream come true. Nothing would be out of his reach now. Halstrom's Team would consist of superhuman soldiers. No one would stand in his way again. Any who dared to get between him and his goals would pay the price. He listened as his men moved out.

Satisfied that all was going as planned, he made ready, preparing the container to hold his prize. It was just about then he heard new voices not far ahead and to the side of his convoy. Voices he recognized.

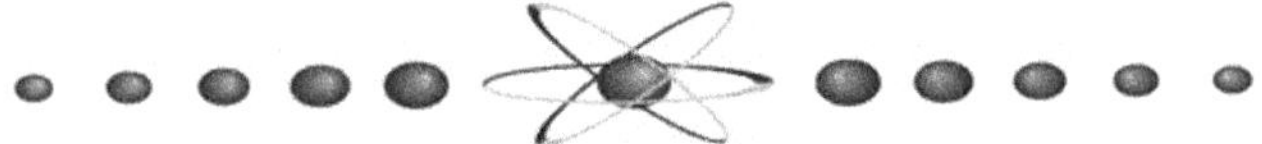

Keri cried out as her device began to smoke, "What the heck was that?"

James replied, "I think Timothy knows we're here."

As their SUV came to a sudden halt, James began mobilizing the teams, sending them ahead with orders not to harm the target. As they move out, James tells Keri to stay behind, out of harm's way. Keri watches as they move into the fog, disappearing as if by magic, sucked into the smoke of the landscape. Keri was worried that something might go wrong. Timothy might hurt their friends. She couldn't bare that thought, knowing it would be all her fault. She took a deep breath, steadying herself against the fear. That didn't last long as she began to hear gunshots ahead in the thick fog. That wasn't her team's weapons, she was sure of it. That was live fire. She knew the difference right off.

She surmised that others must be there, but the sounds were more like battle and there were many of them. This wasn't some stray hunter, this was military weapons, no doubt about it. Now Keri was getting very concerned. She drew her stun baton just in case, moving to the front of the SUV. Her radio began to show chatter again. The lights on the dash of the SUV came on, she could clearly see the digital readout on the dash pad as she walked forward. The fog had only gotten thicker though, making it very difficult to see ahead. She stopped as she reached the front tire, not wanting to step away from the only protection she had out in the open like this.

She heard a noise behind her, turning she could make out the silhouette of a very tall man. Then as it continued to advance on her position, she noticed it wasn't a normal man's image at all. It was way too tall for a normal person. Pushing her stun baton out in front of her, readying herself against anything that might come, she stood her ground. Her hand holding the baton suddenly went limp, causing the baton to point downward. It was Timothy. He was making his way toward her slowly, as if he recognized her. She heard him sniffing the air, his large eyes pushing into her as he drew closer and closer.

She heard her name, "Waaattttzzz."

Timothy stopped. Keri slowly moved forward, closing the distance between them. Tears were pouring down her cheeks, her heart about to burst. She slowly reached up to touch his face.

He spoke her name again, "Waaaattttzzzz."

She quietly said, "Yes, it's me Timothy. I'm so sorry. I had to do it. You were dying. I had to save you. I didn't know this would happen. Please forgive me."

She leaned in to wrap her arms around him. She felt his arms embrace her. She looked up into his eyes, seeing recognition and sadness. She knew he forgave her. She could tell he understood what was happening.

"Timothy, we have to get you out of here, get you to safety while we figure out how to fix this. We need to go."

She released Timothy, pulling the radio off her belt she called to James, "recall the teams James, Timothy is here with me."

She heard James acknowledge her. She slid her arms around Timothy's waist, holding him closely. Feeling his arms around her again. She was just enjoying the moment when suddenly she felt something impact Timothy's back. Then several more as she felt Timothy pushing her away, turning to face whatever had hit him. That's when she watched as General Halstrom stepped out of the fog with a rifle in his hands. She watched as Timothy went down to his knees as General Halstrom shot him again in the chest. There were a number of tranq darts sticking out of his back. Keri could feel the anger welling up from within.

"You bastard! It was you all along wasn't it?"

Halstrom smiled, "Yes, it was me. I shut you down. I took all your specimens, everything. It's all mine now. And so is he. He is Government Property now."

Halstrom aimed the rifle at Keri, his finger tensing as he was talking. Keri was ready. When he fired the shot at her, she lept to the side, flinging her stun baton at his weapon. Then launching herself at him to disarm him. By the time he recovered enough to attempt another shot, Keri was on him like a crazed mother cat protecting her kittens. Only this mama cat was like a ninja, knocking the weapon from his hands, she laid a nimble knee to the midsection, sending him reeling backwards. But General Halstrom was well versed in the arts of hand to hand combat.

"You'll pay for that little girl. I think I'll take you with us, along with your green friend there.

Maybe turn you into one of my super-soldiers also. I'm curious as to see what a female hybrid would look like. I bet the transformation would be truly astounding."

As Keri side stepped a few of his approaches, preparing to launch another attack, his words began to anger her more and more. She wasn't prepared for his quick movements though. He was much faster than should be possible. Leering down on her as he circled around her. He feigned one direction and caught her by surprise with a midsection punch. The force of it put her on her back. Just as he stepped up to kick her in the head, she swept his feet, spinning around and up onto her feet again. Proving her skills were to be feared. She moved in quickly, throwing a blow to the throat that should have put him down. But his reflexes were fast, causing his hand to make it a glancing blow. While he choked a bit, he moved into a defensive stance while he recovered.

Keri was boiling angry at him, "So you planned it all didn't you? I bet you put the hit on Timothy too, didn't you?"

Halstrom smiled again, "He wouldn't play ball. I sent a team to invite him to bring you back onboard. I needed him to get to you. Every time I asked you to join us, you refused. We found references to the formula but no data. You had it hidden away. Someone had let it slip in the records that you had created a formula which had wonderful effects on some rat. But we couldn't find anything in the database about it. It was your little secret. How were we to know you had kept it at the old location, hidden in some back storage room refrigerator, right under our very noses. But Timothy decided to play hero and pulled a weapon. My team were a bit edgy and you saw what happened after that. I don't blame them. Timothy is one formidable foe. Now he will be under my control."

He had been trying to put Keri at ease and chose that exact moment to feign tripping on a small branch under his feet. Keri, seeing him appear to go off balance, rushed in for a strike, only to watch as Halstrom quickly slid under her aimed blow to land a hit right in the center of Keri's chest, knocking the wind out of her, putting her down. As she hit the dirt hard, Halstrom stood over her sending his boots into her midsection several times, ensuring his victory.

Keri felt each blow, watching as spit flew from her mouth, feeling the pain shoot through her whole body. Looking across into Timothy's unconscious face, knowing she had lost the battle. Watching as light faded to have the darkness close in. Another boot pulled back, anticipating the blow, hearing a grunt instead. Keri's last effort rolled her head just enough to hear a body fall, causing dust to sail in all directions. As she watched the dust shoot past her blurry vision, a boot stepped forward. Putting all she could muster into turning her head upward, she could barely make out Aidra standing over Halstrom with Keri's stun baton in hand. Then the darkness closed in, embracing her mind where she smiled, feeling comforted with the understanding that Timothy was safe after all. She was safe too. Keri could rest, so she did, falling into oblivion.

Keri could hear voices now. A man and woman. They appeared to be talking about her condition. Everything appeared to be ok besides some bruises. That's not how she felt though.

"Did anyone get the license of that truck that hit me?" Keri said, as she opened her eyes to see James and Dr. Hope Songe standing by her bed.

Keri chuckled as she finished her joke. James came directly to her bedside, eyeing her with concern. Keri tried to sit up but thought better of it as nausea swept over her.

"You sit tight girl. You took some nasty hits to the midsection. You should not be moving at all for a day or two. I don't want to see any more of that for now. Do you hear me?" James commanded.

"Yes Sir!" Keri curtly replied, as she tried to raise her arm to salute. It was too sore to lift very far so she just lowered it down, settling for a smartass response.

Remembering Timothy, Keri sat up quickly. Feeling like she was going to puke, she laid back in a sitting position.

"Where's Timothy? Is he ok? Did we bring him in?"

James helped her sit back as he explained that all was well, "Timothy took a number of tranqs. He's been out of it. Other than that, he seems to be in very good shape. Nothing bad whatsoever to show for the whole ordeal."

Keri noticed her midsection was bandaged as she moved her legs to the edge.

"I'm getting up James, just get out of my way please. I'm not going to lay here when Timothy could come around at any moment. All of this could be for nothing if he flees again. Not to mention the mess he could make of this building." Keri was looking at her surroundings, "Where are we anyway?"

She looked at James and then Hope for an answer.

James said, "We're at a safehouse where General Halstrom can't find us. I've had this place for several years now. You never know when some place like this might come in handy. Especially when you work for the government in their secret projects."

James stepped back, knowing better than to try to stop Keri once she had her mind made up. Keri was stubborn sometimes. Not someone to toy with once they make their desires known. He did help her up though. Keri made her way to Timothy's room nearby. Hope brought her a pain killer.

"Thanks for patching me up Hope." Keri mumbled.

"Not a problem girl. Luckily for you, it's not that bad. Nothing broken, except maybe your pride. A few deeper bruises, but you'll be fine in a few days."

Keri nodded her head, giving Hope a hug before she sat down beside Timothy.

"Where's everyone at?" Keri asked.

Hope replied, "James sent them all home. Told them all to go on alert status for the next week while he figures out our next move."

Keri nodded her head, "Good thinking on James' part. Halstrom will be looking for us. We'll have to lay low until we can figure things out."

James entered the room just then, "No need to worry about that. I have a surprise for you Keri. Meet Mr. Jay Bravo."

Keri watched as Jay walked into the room, reached out his hand expecting Keri to take his. He stood about 5'8" 140 lbs with slicked back black hair held neatly in a ponytail going down to his shoulders, wearing nothing more than common looking clothes. Other than his sturdy handsome features, nothing stood out of place about him. Keri looked him up and down, refusing to take his hand.

"Why is there a mister Jay Bravo standing in front of me James?" Keri said as she looked past Jay seeking an answer from James.

James walked up beside Jay, who had lowered his hand by this time but decided to interrupt what James was about to explain. As Jay began to speak in an authoritative manner, causing Keri to shift her gaze to lock eyes with Jay, a stern look began to form on Keri's face, plainly showing her irritation.

"I called James to inform him that I would be taking over funding of your little operation here. Seeing as how you have bungled things a bit. I thought I would help you fix it. Not to mention getting General Halstrom off your asses. That took some heavy string pulling just now. He won't be bothering you for a while."

Keri looked like she would spit nails just then. "What do you mean, take over the funding of our little operation? Who the hell do you think you are?"

James decided to step in between them. "Keri, this is Jay Bravo, the multi-billionaire. He has a bit of a problem in which he needs our help and we can sure use his help right about now. It just so happens that he has been following your research for a long time now and all the security systems in our old building just so happen to be his as it was his funding which kept things under the books on our project. At least until General Halstrom shut us down. That building belongs to Jay here. So when you reopened the building to help Timothy, Jay just so happened to receive notices of our use of the facility automatically. Yet he chose to leave us to our own without bothering us. But now, he decided to step forward to help us. Just listen to his story, I think you'll be rather surprised. Fact is, I know you will be. There's no way in hell you're going to walk away from this."

Then James stepped back, motioning for Jay to finish the story. Jay nodded his head slightly in appreciation to James for helping him, then turned to Keri.

"Dr. Watts, I've been following your work for years. As James just explained, I'm the owner of the facility you have been working at all this time. Our project was a joint D.O.D. and military cooperative. Off the books of course, but nonetheless a government black ops project. When Senator Owens died, General Halstrom stepped in. When he got wind of my facilities under Senator Owens guidance, he decided to take over all the assets. That's when you got shut down. I have been following your work in hoping that it might help a friend of mine. That's why I funded the operation. Your work with the rat is what really got my attention. Then what happened with Timothy. That's when I decided to open another facility. This one was done in secret however. Not even the government knows of its existence and I want you to run it."

Keri cut in just then, "Why would I work for you Mr. Bravo? What makes you think I would want anything to do with you or your secret operation?"

James interrupted, "Keri, let him finish his story. He hasn't even gotten to the best part yet. So please, just hear him out."

Keri crossed her arms, "Go ahead Mr. Bravo. I'm curious to hear this story James keeps referring to. I can't wait to hear this." She said with pure disdain in her voice.

Jay cleared his throat, took a deep breath and then continued his explanation. "Well, about a year ago, a friend of mine, Jason Locke, asked me to help him investigate some paranormal activity on an island off the coast of Africa, way off the coast. Fact is it didn't show up on any maps that we could find and I have vast resources but still no map. Well, as you can imagine, my interest was piqued. So we decided to take a bit of a vacation and check out this island. There had been many stories of orb like lights zipping around this island over the years. Some of the stories were reported to be hundreds of years old but now there were new stories being told from very recent times.

"So we loaded into one of my larger yachts, headed that way. We figured we would enjoy a nice vacation and do some spelunking as well. Everything was going well until about the third day on the island. While the island was only about twelve miles in length and a good four miles wide, that is still a rather large area to cover. We had just about finished surveying the whole island, not finding anything out of the ordinary, when that night some lights showed up right about in the center of the island. We set out to explore the area, which we had somehow managed to miss as it turns out. It was rather difficult since it was dark out. There were animals on the island, we had found, so we had to be careful. Most of the dangerous ones were snakes, as you can imagine. But as we got closer to the area, we could make out a number of lights. It appeared to be coming from just ahead. We figured it must be pirates or something. You know in that part of the world there are many stories of pirates, with none of them pleasant.

"So we decided to be very cautious. I had my .45 on me and Jason had his 9mm. We felt safe enough. But when we got about a hundred yards from the lights, they shot right up into the sky. Pretty much instantly and they were miles away. I'm not sure what it was but I have my suspicions. Especially after following your past work. Anyways, this is when things got a bit nasty. We figured we had just seen a UFO, of course. So we decided to move on in to the area where it had just been. See if they left any signs of their having been there. We didn't make it very far when we began to hear howls. Like wolf howls."

Keri laughed, then interrupted Jay, "Don't tell me? Werewolves, right?"

Jay looked at James for a moment, then back to Keri. Jay slowly nodded his head. Keri held her hand up between her and Jay to stop him as Jay was just about to begin his story again.

"Hold up there a minute. You're telling me there were Werewolves on this island? You've got to be kidding me. James, where did you find this guy? Is this some kind of sick joke?"

She looked at James with a disgusted expression. But Jay just turned around, ignoring Keri, and called out behind him, "Jason, would you mind coming in here for a minute?"

Jason Locke entered the room. He stood around 6' tall, all muscles, with spiked shoulder length black hair, and scruffy like facial hair. You would have thought a regular ole body builder had walked in, with his tanned complexion, he had strange yet commanding presence like you wouldn't take your eyes off of him. This was no normal man.

He strolled up to Jay's side, simply stated, "Yea Jay, what's up?"

A smile widened across Jay's face, "This is Jason. As you can see, he is not your normal person. You can tell just being in his presence that he is different. He exudes grace and dominance. His stare will turn your will to mush. His touch will turn your drive to weakness."

Then Jay turned to Jason, "Jason, would you be so kind as to shift into form for the good doctor here. She needs to know everything if she is to help us."

Jason didn't bat an eye, "Sure thing Jay, everyone please do not touch me once I shift. My reflexes are so sharp that sometimes I move before I realize what I have done. So stand very still for me, no sudden movements."

As everyone stepped back a few steps, giving Jason plenty of room. Jason bowed his head, then it was as if his whole body shuddered and began to strain against his own skin. Everyone noticed a lot of heat coming off him as his form began to shift with sudden eruptions of crunching bones or tearing skin which seemed to fade right before their very eyes as hair sprouted all over his body. His clothes fell to the floor, shredded in tatters of rags. When he lifted his head again, all they saw was an elongated snout of a wild beast with teeth so big you could swear they would snap you in half without any effort on his part. The rest of his body was bulging beast muscle and long dark hair. It felt like he was immitting a gravity wave or something. Like you were being pulled towards him. Everyone had to resist the urge to fall to him. It was strange to say the least.

Jay spoke, causing Jason's head to jerk his direction. Jason's movement was so fast, it was a blur. What happened next took everyone by surprise. A flash of green suddenly appeared between Keri and Jason, followed by a roar of outworldly noise. Jason's shift into the beast must have triggered Timothy. It was a fearsome sight, Timothy pushed Keri behind him as he roared. Everyone fell backwards suddenly except Jason. In a flash of mixed colors, Jason was on Timothy. But Timothy was holding his own, as he had Jason by the wrists, dodging Jason's bites. Keri was knocked backwards into the wall.

If not for what happened next, there's no telling what would have happened. Jay triggered some type of device. It was loud, some kind of handheld thing but it sounded like a horn or something. Timothy and Jason stopped their struggles instantly. Jason took the moment to jump away from Timothy towards the doorway. You could tell by the look on Jason's face, even though it was a beast to be sure, that he was trying to clear his mind. Timothy held his ground, unmoving. You could begin to see sparks flying off the fins on his back. But Keri got up and rushed to Timothy, moving past him to get between him and Jason. Looking up into Timothy's eyes she began to plead with him to calm down. Jason slipped out of the room so quickly you wondered if he had ever even been there to begin with. Just a blur of fur and glinting specks from his teeth and nails flash out the door.

Keri was getting through to Timothy who was breathing heavily from his exertion, but clearly calming down. Timothy looked around the room, from one person to the next.

They all heard him say, "Waaatttzzz." as he turned his attention back to Keri, looking down at her he pulled her close.

Keri reached up, touching Timothy on the face, smiling, yet a tear was running down her cheek. They heard a scream down the hallway, which caused Timothy to react, pushing Keri behind him again. Facing the doorway, readying for anything. Jay eased out the door, keeping an eye on Timothy as he cautiously left the room. James followed just behind Jay, glancing back at Timothy as he exited the room. They found Dr. Songe unconscious on the floor with Jason nowhere in site. Jay went past Dr. Songe's still form calling to Jason. James stopped to check on Dr. Songe. She seemed fine, no damage or anything. She must've passed out from the shock of seeing a Werewolf running through the hallway.

James mumbled, "Just another day in paradise", as he went to get smelling salts out of the med kit."

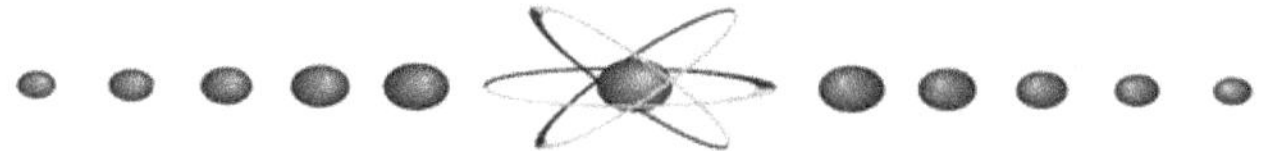

6 months later…

Dr. Keri Watts was bent over her desk reviewing the last few months progress. Using Jason's blood and Timothy's combined with more of the serum she had given Timothy to save his life, she was making progress on correcting Timothy's mutation. She felt she was getting close now. Jason's blood had an unusual virus in it. She had concluded that one of the alien species were running tests here on earth and abandoning test subjects on that island. She had sent James with

Jason back to the island to retrieve one of the wolves which had bitten Jason. They were pretty much just regular wolves with some differences. The aliens had obviously injected the wolves with some type of virus which had only slightly mutated to give them larger muscle mass and a few other changes. Other than that, you couldn't tell them apart from normal wolves. They did appear to be able to see a bit better at night and smell things further away than the normal wolf. Their healing was a bit accelerated also. Not a lot of changes but enough. Why they had just dumped them on the island though? Maybe they were going to check backup on them later to see if they had mutated or something. Keri wasn't sure.

Everyone had been transported to their new facilities. Located underground in Australia, they were off the radar of Halstrom now. Drake, Coyote, Aidra, James, and Dr. Songe were all here. Felt like old times again. Timothy's old team, back together. Timothy had calmed down and his memories were nearly all restored. All except the night he nearly died, he still couldn't remember that. Keri knew that Timothy was sneaking out at night, hunting. His base instincts were troubling him a bit causing him to crave the outdoors. His senses were so sharp now. He was the main supplier of meat. He would go out, track down game, bring it back with only a few pieces missing. She smiled as she thought about it all. Then she couldn't help herself as a tear would find its way forward, clouding her vision. She knew Timothy's condition was all her fault. She also knew that she was going to be the one to fix it.

Timothy could use plain english again. He kept telling her to stop worrying about his condition. He felt wonderful, powerful. He seemed to like everything except when he looked in the mirror. He had gotten so upset early on that he had broken the mirror in his room. But later he asked for it to be replaced. So he was getting used to his new appearance. She would fix that, she was sure of it. She was so close to a breakthrough. Dr. Songe was working on Jason's problem. Yet much of the time they spent discussing the similarities of the two. She would share a bit of data concerning her tests and Dr. Songe would suddenly relate some fact from hers and it seemed to help them both. So there was similar problems with both cases. The DNA makeup were very similar in some ways. Fact is recently, Keri had taken some samples of Dr. Songe's to use in her experiments. Something about the virus in Jason allowed progress as she sought to isolate what had caused Timothy to mutate his form. A bit longer and she felt there would be a cure or at least headway.

Today, Jay had showed up with new information on Sparks. It appeared that General Halstrom had Sparks locked away on some base that wasn't listed as a base. While he was being experimented on, he healed fast so while Keri was sure it wasn't pleasant, Jay assured her he was alive and surviving. Halstrom appeared to have another black ops project probably. But who was overseeing this one? Either he was partnered with some government ABC group or some senator had him under his thumb. Either way, it didn't matter.

They were going to break Sparks out. When she had worked with Sparks in the past, he was actually willing to help her. It was like he felt paternal of her and other humans. Like he felt responsible for humans. He kept saying his group had been watching over our planet, keeping other aliens from interfering with us. But we got shut down by Halstrom before I could look into that. If that was true, then Sparks could help them. Maybe they could help Sparks. Give him back his freedom or something. Keri liked that idea. She didn't enjoy treating him like a lab rat before. Fact is she had made sure he was treated with respect in every way possible. At least as far as she was allowed at the time. Which wasn't much.

So they had determined a plan by nightfall. Jay had gotten his hands on maps and diagrams of Halstrom's facility. He wouldn't say how, but Keri was sure it had something to do with a lot of zeros on someone's bank account. Keri didn't care, as long as they got Sparks out of Halstrom's hands.

Genetic Nightmare

CHAPTER SIX

Growing up can be tough...

Learning What Family Means

Santiago woke. As he opened his eyes expecting to wake up dead, the throbbing pain shot through his eyes into the back of his head bringing nausea full force against his midsection. Quicky closing his eyes after noticing he was indoors, Santiago laid back relaxing. Knowing the only way to make progress was by releasing the tension. He slowly opened his eyes again, this time clearly making out his own bedroom.

Before he could stop himself, Santiago swore out loud, *what the hell?*

Santiago could do nothing but close his eyes as the nausea swept over him again. Surprisingly, nothing came out. Trying to relax again, Santiago slowly opened his eyes not wanting to cause another wave of sickness to invade his mind. He could hear someone coming up the stairs. It sounded like Isabella but he couldn't be sure. How he could possibly be here after what happened in the jungle was too much for his mind to process.

The shock of it held him still while he waited to see who would step into the room to confront him. He tried to convince himself that it had to be a dream. There was no other explanation that he could even entertain right then.

As Isabella entered the room, Santiago began to realize that the impossible had happened. He was back home when he should be dead. A miracle had transpired and his mind could find no explanation for it. Yet Isabella began to explain exactly what happened. Matias, my brother, had been on his way to visit when a large cat had crossed his path. He was tracking it as it made its way around my ranch.

Matias had not mentioned anything about Pike. The panther had run off when Santiago had taken a strike to the side of the head, making enough noise to scare off the large cat. Santiago looked down at **Valedor** who was silently watching his every move as if he was concerned for his welfare. Santiago reached out to stroke his neck assuring him that all was well. Isabella had made something to eat for Matias who was downstairs still.

It was late evening now, the construction crews had all cleared out and Matias had gone. Santiago was just about to make the attempt to go downstairs when he saw Valedor suddenly shift his view to the upstairs bedroom window. Isabella noticed also, moving to the window, she let out a sudden gasp as Santiago watched Pike suddenly appear there looking in. Opening the window, Isabella let Pike in. Without scolding him, she wrapped his small form in her arms where Pike clung in a loving embrace of affection. All the while Pike was staring at him with a look of concern. Santiago moved over to put his arms around Isabella and Pike. His family was all here, safe. Everything was back to normal. Valedor decided to muscle in on the affection as he pushed in between them to lick Pike on the side of the face. Pike appeared to smile as he reached up to touch Valedor, stroking down the side of his head.

Six Months Later...

Over the last six months Pike had sprouted like a leaf. He now stood at a good seven feet in height. They had taught Pike to speak spanish and english. He was a very fast learner. During that time, Pike had learned to adjust well to keeping out of sight but also he kept the jungle around the ranch clear of all predators which might cause them problems.

Several months back Santiago had finally given Pike the box which they had pulled from the Alien spaceship the day they had found Pike. Santiago had never figured out how to open the box. It wasn't large by any means but there didn't appear to be any way of opening it. Even when he had tried to use his power tools on it, he couldn't even scratch the surface. It was like it was indestructible. When Pike finally took interest in it, Santiago decided to let him have it. Pike was having trouble opening it also. It was keeping Pike occupied lately, which was a good thing. Isabella had mentioned that Pike was getting a bit impatient about things as if he craved to be off on adventures. Isabella had returned to her normal self during the last six months also. It was a great relief to Santiago to have his love behaving normal again.

It was very interesting how things had changed in their life. Knowing that Pike was an alien yet also knowing that he was like a son to them. Or more importantly, he was their son. He could not imagine what it would be like not to have

Pike for his son. Life would not be worth living any longer if something were to happen to Pike. It was unthinkable. Santiago watched as Pike toyed with the box. Rubbing it on its sides and bottom, pushing, scratching, slapping it. Nothing seemed to work.

Finally I decided to try to help him, "Pike, maybe you should try using your mind. Your thoughts to open it. After all, it comes from your people and we are not familiar with how that technology works."

Pike replied, "Father, you make a good suggestion. I'll temper my patience and attempt to use my mind capacities to affect it."

Santiago nodded in agreement as Pike calmed himself. Holding the box in his hands, Pike closed his eyes and relaxed. Santiago smiled, thinking how intelligent Pike was. He was so smart. Santiago was amazed by him so often. It was almost more than he could bare thinking about it. Sometimes tears would form at the corners of his eyes as he contemplated how blessed he and Isabella were to have him for their son. As Santiago watched his son concentrate, he noticed the box in Pike's hands begin to glow. Shaking off the mesmerizing effect of the moment, Santiago kept quiet, not wanting to interrupt what was taking place.

Something was happening. Pike was making progress. He had no idea what was inside of the box but knew that Pike would be the one to find out. It was like destiny in his mind, only Pike could walk this path. Santiago found himself smiling now. The glow was increasing in intensity. He was sure that Pike must be sensing this. He could feel it on his own skin similar to sunlight warming you when you stepped outdoors.

Pike spoke, "Father, I can hear it. It speaks to me. It is very powerful, I can tell. I don't know what to ask of it Father. What should I tell it?"

Santiago was reluctant to direct Pike but understood that Pike looked up to him for wisdom. With that in mind Santiago formulated what he considered a wise approach.

Santiago replied, "It would be wise to ask it to provide you with guidelines on how to proceed I would think son. Ask it for options."

"Very wise indeed father."

Santiago watched as Pike concentrated harder. Then suddenly the box opened. Pike reached into the box, took out what appeared to be a diadem. Pike opened his eyes to look upon it as he placed it on his head. The diadem was glowing so brightly that you could not make out much about it other than it appeared to be made of some form of metal. Yet it continually seemed to change form in subtle ways, as if it was alive maybe. Santiago couldn't tell. As Pike placed the diadem on his head his eyes began to glow also. A blank expression formed on Pike's face momentarily.

Pike spoke, "Don't worry father. I am interfacing with this device. It is increasing the neural paths which allow faster speeds of my thinking processes. It's also sharing knowledge with me but only doing as I instruct it. Very cool father."

Santiago watched as Pike appeared to be interacting with the device in some fashion. Santiago was a bit concerned for Pike's safety but knew that the device he was using was from his own kind. More than that, he trusted Pike's decisions. He knew Pike would not be doing something that was not clearly understood in his own mind. So this device must be providing a lot of information to him. Strange how things like that worked yet Santiago understood oh so well.

The technology available today that interfaced with the human form on many levels was astounding. So something like this of even higher technology from Pike's people was not surprising to him in the least. He would trust Pike's judgements on the matter. Then just as all seemed well, Pike suddenly shifted his view. His head tilted upward and to the side as if he could see through the wall into the sky. Santiago could tell by the expression forming on Pike's face that something was wrong.

"What is it son?"

"Father, the device is showing me a warning. It appears that by activating this device, a being in another galaxy far far away has been notified of its location. The device is warning me as if it was a bad thing. I have asked for information on the being that has detected my device."

Suddenly Pike snatched the device from his head, pushing it back into the box as the light from it went out quickly. Pike slammed the lid shut. The expression on Pike's face was one Santiago had seen before. The kind a young one makes when they realize a grave mistake has been made.

"Father, I'm afraid. I think I have made a horrible mistake."

"Santiago asked, "Why do you say that son?"

Pike looked at Santiago with fear in his eyes, "They are coming father. When I activated it I had ignored the suggested protocols it had laid out. I should have followed the directions but I was impatient to see what it could do. When it showed me the menu options of increasing fluid intelligence that were a normal part of my people, of course I told it to proceed. Since I did not have it put up a resonance shield, a signal was emitted through space. Now they will come. They are very bad. This is not good father."

Then something else took place with Pike. His eyes began to glow again. His gaze shifted to the side as if he could see far away.

Sparks could sense them coming to rescue him. As soon as they drew within a few miles of his location, he knew their intentions. Sparks was in a weakened condition from all the experiments that were being performed on him. Even with his fast healing their invasive and destructive tests were doing more and more damage to his body. If he could have escaped, he would have months ago and while he had one opportunity to do just that, he would have had to kill the only one here who had shown him kindness. He could not bring himself to do that. He fully understood how humans thought. With Spark's longevity, a few years imprisoned by humans was nothing he couldn't handle. At least that was his first thought process concerning his situation. Yet with these new doctors and this new facility of research, he wasn't so sure.

Then just at that moment Spark's eyes began to glow as his gaze shifted to one side as if he could see through the laboratory wall.

Sparks exclaimed, "My son, you are alive!"

The End

Watch for Book Two of the Bio Wars Saga...

ABOUT THE AUTHORS

Timothy is the original creator of the story Genetic Nightmare. The duo work together to further share and advance the world that Timothy envisioned. Husband and father of two, Timothy spends his time supporting his family and expanding his mind. Enjoying all the wonderful diversity of literary endeavors, Timothy shares his ideas freely with those around him. His love for gaming and adventure have always been his strong points bringing his creativity to the forefront. Timothy was born in Kansas and as he learned to read he loved to research and read about all things paranormal

as best as he could to envision how such creatures and all things paranormal could exist in our reality. As timothy began high school he began to create his characters and formulated over their depiction for years before meeting mark and embarking on the adventure of creating the genetic nightmare series bringing all things paranormal under one roof and one universe. As Timothy grew older he had a mindset keep an open mind ask questions and just think of a way to make things work for your reality and as you will come to find out the impossible can seem probable.

Guy's writing has been called pure genius by many. Some say his writing can be overly complex at times but well worth the reading. It stems from his life of studies in physics and philosophy, having spent much time working with potential dimensional realities moving beyond the 3d in conceptual consciousness. This, along with his purported extra-ordinary experiences, explain his insight into other dimensional realities and the beings that one might encounter there.

Guy grew up in the small towns of Oklahoma, raising horses in his back yard. Getting up early before *school to ride his favorite mare named Raven gives him warm memories still. It was later after marrying and starting a family of three kids that he opened his book store. His favorite hobby was reading and before he knew it he had read over 500 books.*

His favorite genre was fantasy series. Mix in a couple hundred adventure and western novels to round things out. Soon he was writing novels himself. Later he began to produce and direct film projects. If you looked in his house today you would find right in his front room a green screen studio along with his desk and computer system where he spends so much time writing and working on film edits or special effects software. In the last year he produced over twenty music videos alone, not to mention many other videos he has produced associated with movie production projects.

He prides himself on taking his time to personally communicate with all his fans. One of his main points he makes to those that know him, "Always treat others the way you want to be treated." Searching the internet for famous quotes, you can find Guy quoted a number of times. Guy's favorite is "The ripples we make today turn into the waves of change tomorrow."

Guy also spends much of his time working on community projects in the arts. Sitting on the board of a local non-profit, Guy gets to meet many actors, directors and producers, as well as, politicians now and then. You can find Guy at events autographing books or doing photo shoots with fans.

Reach out to Guy and say hi as he always makes time to reach back out. His personal email is finalter@hotmail.com.

Genetic Nightmare

"Please go to Amazon.com and leave a review of our book. You can't imagine how much it helps and we need all the help we can get. <smile>...Thank you." --Guy Lozier & Timothy Gibbs